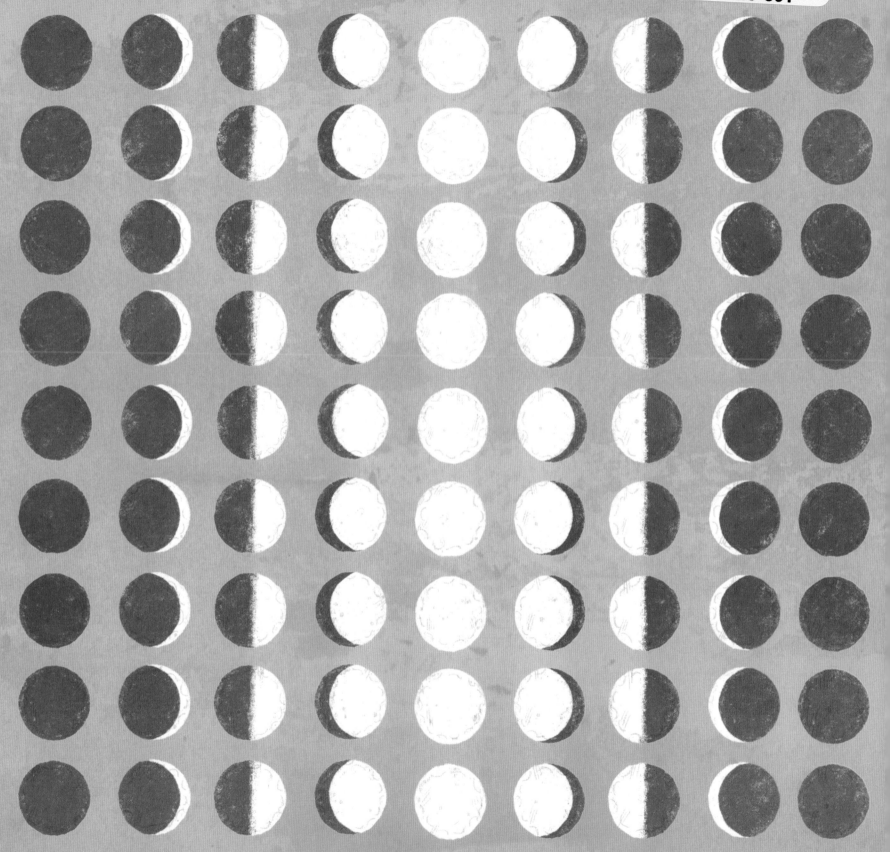

To Farshid, Kian, and Zayn

Versify® is an imprint of HarperCollins Publishers.

Moon's Ramadan
Copyright © 2023 by Natasha Khan Kazi
All rights reserved. Manufactured in Italy. No part of this book may be used or reproduced
in any manner whatsoever without written permission except in the case of brief quotations
embodied in critical articles and reviews. For information address HarperCollins Children's Books,
a division of HarperCollins Publishers, 195 Broadway, New York, NY 10007.
www.harpercollinschildrens.com

ISBN 978-0-35-869409-0

The artist used scanned watercolor textures and digital pencils to create the illustrations for this book.
Typography by Whitney Leader-Picone
22 23 24 25 26 RTLO 10 9 8 7 6 5 4 3 2 1

First Edition

MOON'S RAMADAN

Natasha Khan Kazi

▼ VERSIFY | *An Imprint of HarperCollinsPublishers*

In the purple veil of twilight, Moon smiles at Earth.
Her sliver of silver signals the start of Ramadan, a month of peace.
Moon peeks through paper pennants and tin-plated fawanees.
Hands point toward her new crescent.
Moon is excited too.

"Hello!" Moon calls.
She wants to celebrate too.
But people rush inside.
Homes must be swept and scrubbed to sparkle,
warm and inviting like Moon.

EGYPT

Badoom! Badoom!
Before sunrise, the drummer's barrel booms.
Moon listens to the beat as dozy eyes wake up from sleep.
It's time for Suhoor, the early morning meal.

TURKEY

Those of the right age and health will fast.
During daylight, no food or drink will pass their lips.

Their hands will only do good deeds.
Their mouths will only speak kind words.
Always thinking of those who have less.

Every night, Moon travels around the world, observing Ramadan.
After sunset, families gather for Iftar, a meal to break the fast.
They begin with a cool glass of water and a plump date.
With gratitude and patience, they fill their plates.
Savory smells waft out windows.

Moon shares a greeting,
"Ramadan Kareem!"

INDONESIA

As each day passes, Moon grows fuller, happily watching children do good deeds. Even the smallest hands make a big difference.

They deliver baskets filled with sweet dried fruit
and honey-soaked pastries.
Moon spies half-moon cookies, black and white, too.
"I will light your way," Moon says.

UNITED KINGDOM

In the purple veil of twilight,
Moon smiles at Earth.

Leaders wax lyrical, speaking
warmly about zakat, charity
during Ramadan.

NEW ZEALAND

Moon waxes too, growing larger every night,
as families share their wealth with those in need.

Clink, clank, clunk!
Children drop coins into sadaqah jars.
Moon wishes she could
share her shiny moon rocks.

Then, when Moon shines full and bright,
one beautiful voice calls all inside.
It's time for Taraweeh, the nightly prayer
during Ramadan.

SOMALIA

The Imam, who leads worshipers, will recite
from the Islamic holy book, the Quran.
Moon's perfect circle signals that
Ramadan is half done.

Moon marvels as friends of different faiths share a meal to celebrate.
Together, they rise like bread.
Tonight neighbors break biscuits, challah, naan, and pita.
Sliced for sharing, the bread is Moon's last quarter shape.

UNITED STATES

The scent of muddy, silky henna drifts above.
Moon spins happily to see the swoop of her
waning crescent painted on palms
as a row of hands waits.

"How do I look?" Moon asks.
Little hands are busy drying.
Smiles mirror Moon's crescent.

DUBAI

In the purple veil of twilight,
Moon magically melts into mulberry and lavender hues.
Below her, people search the sky.

"I'm here!" Moon calls.
But there is no answer.
Feet shuffle back inside.

ARGENTINA

"You can't see me, but I am always here for you."
Her lunar month is ending.

Moon is new.

Moon's sliver of silver signals a new month is beginning.
Moon is sad to see Ramadan end.

But then she spots a twinkle, and light begins to spread . . .

Moon beams with joy as people light lanterns
to celebrate Chaand Raat, the night of the moon.
And Moon remembers, Ramadan is over, but tomorrow is Eid.

The celebration is not over yet.

INDIA

"Eid Mubarak!" "Happy Eid!"

Moon hears a chorus of calls as people share warm embraces and little ones gleefully count the money in their Eidi.

"Eid Mubarak! Happy Eid!" Moon calls.

EGYPT

And in the purple veil of twilight . . .

a billion faces smile up at Moon.
Moon sees a world of love and kindness,
and she glows with gratitude.

Eidi envelopes

Ramadan cookies

gifts for neighbors

AUTHOR'S NOTE

Did you know there are over 1.8 billion Muslims globally? Islam, the religion practiced by Muslims, is the second-largest religion in the world. The month of Ramadan, which ends with the Eid al-Fitr holiday, is the most important time for the Muslim community. It is a time for Muslims to renew their spirits by doing acts of kindness, giving to charity, and fasting.

THE LUNAR CYCLE

Ramadan is the ninth month in the Islamic calendar. Unlike the most commonly used calendar, the Gregorian calendar, which is based on the sun's position, the Islamic calendar is based on the lunar cycle, the moon's journey around the earth. Since the lunar month is approximately 29.5 days, and shorter than the Gregorian month, Ramadan shifts 11 days earlier every year. In one lifetime, you could celebrate Ramadan in the winter and the summer!

Ramadan lantern

moon spotting binoculars

PHASES OF THE MOON

Waxing Crescent   First Quarter   Waxing Gibbous   Full Moon   Waning Gibbous   Last Quarter   Waning Crescent   New Moon

SOURCE

Baby Professor. *The Faces, or Phases, of the Moon: Astronomy Book for Kids.* Children's Astronomy Books. Newark, DE: Speedy Publishing, 2017.

davul (Turkish drum)

henna cone

Islamic crescent moon and star symbol

biscuits   pita   naan   challah

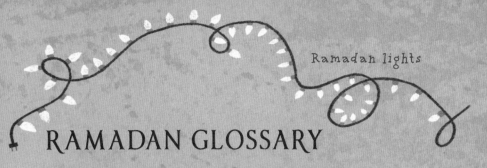
Ramadan lights

prayer rug

RAMADAN GLOSSARY

Chaand Raat: A celebration popular in South Asian communities, Chaand Raat is a festival the night before Eid. It means "night of the moon" in several South Asian languages.

Eid: The celebration after Ramadan is called Eid al-Fitr. Local mosques hold a special Eid prayer in the morning. The rest of the day is spent attending events with family and friends.

Eidi envelopes: It is customary to give money and gifts to children on Eid day. The envelopes that hold the cash are affectionately called Eidi.

Eid Mubarak: The standard greeting on Eid. The Arabic phrase translates to "blessed Eid."

fasting: During Ramadan, Muslims do not drink or eat from dawn to dusk. Muslims fast to strengthen their self-discipline, gratitude, and patience. Children, pregnant women, sick people, and travelers are not required to fast.

fawanees: Tin-plated lanterns that are popular in North Africa and the Middle East.

henna: A special plant-based paste that can be used to temporarily dye skin and hair a reddish-brown color. It is traditional to put henna on one's hands during Ramadan.

Iftar: The meal eaten after sunset to break the daily Ramadan fast.

Imam: An Islamic religious leader.

Islam: A religion based on the Quran and the teachings of Prophet Muhammad (c. 630 CE).

moon spotting: On the first night of Ramadan, Muslims look for the Ramadan Moon, the first sliver of waxing crescent, in the sky.

mosque: The English word for a place of worship for Muslims. The Arabic term is masjid.

Muslim: A person who practices the religion of Islam.

Quran: The holy book of the Islamic religion.

Ramadan decorations: Modern Ramadan decor includes string lights, garlands, wreaths, lanterns, and signage embellished with traditional symbols such as crescent moons, mosques, and lanterns.

Ramadan Drummer: Originating from the Ottoman Empire, the Ramadan Drummer is a musician who bangs a drum to call people to wake up to eat Suhoor. The tradition is still popular in the Middle East.

Ramadan Kareem: The standard greeting during Ramadan. The Arabic phrase translates to "generous Ramadan." You can also wish someone "Ramadan Mubarak," which translates to "blessed Ramadan."

sadaqah jars: Sadaqah is charity given voluntarily. It is popular for children to create sadaqah jars to collect donations.

Suhoor: The pre-dawn meal eaten before fasting.

Taraweeh: The special nightly prayer performed at mosques during Ramadan.

zakat: All Muslims, if they are financially able, are required to donate a percentage of their income each year to charity.

sadaqah jar

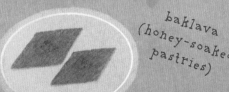
baklava (honey-soaked pastries)

dates

taqiyah or topi (skullcap)

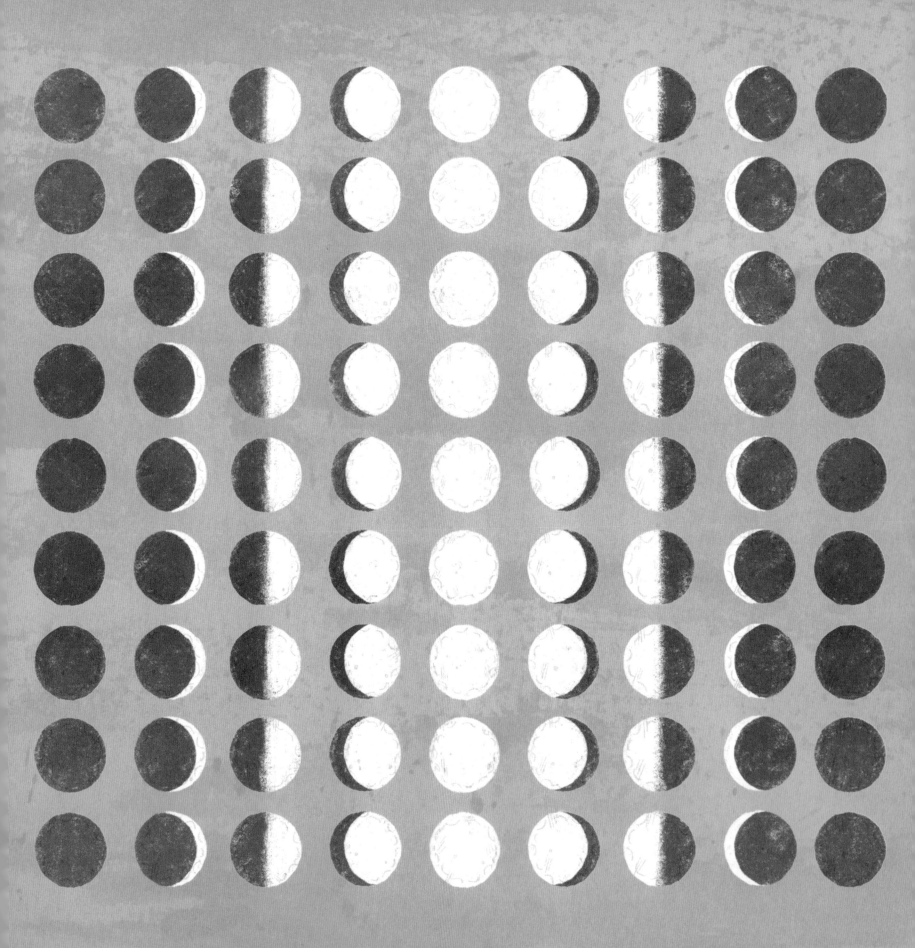